An Ordinary Day

Sally Mitchell Motyka

An Ordinary Day

illustrated by Donna Ayers

Simon and Schuster Books for Young Readers

PUBLISHED BY SIMON & SCHUSTER INC.

NEW YORK

To Julia and Toby
S.M.

To John Gundelfinger
for his criticism and inspiration
D.A.

SIMON AND SCHUSTER BOOKS FOR YOUNG READERS
Simon & Schuster Building, Rockefeller Center, 1230 Avenue of the Americas, New York, N.Y. 10020
Text Copyright © 1989 by Sally Mitchell Motyka. Illustrations Copyright © 1989 by Donna Ayers.
All rights reserved including the right of reproduction in whole or in part in any form.
SIMON AND SCHUSTER BOOKS FOR YOUNG READERS is a trademark of Simon & Schuster Inc.
Manufactured in the United States of America. Designed by Mary Ahern.

10 9 8 7 6 5 4 3 2 1

Library of Congress Cataloging–in–Publication Data: Motyka, Sally Mitchell. An ordinary day.
SUMMARY: Describes the delights of an ordinary day filled with things to touch, taste, see, and enjoy.
[1. Day—Fiction]   I. Ayers, Donna, ill.   II. Title.
PZ7.M85890r   1989 [E]   88-18267
ISBN 0-671-67118-9

It was an ordinary day.

In the morning, the sky was blue.
The air was cool.

The flowers were opening.
The little ants were gathering food.

In the afternoon, the sky was
gray and dark.

The thunder was loud.
The lightning was bright.
The rain was wet.

After the rain, the air was clean and sweet.
A rainbow appeared like magic.

For dinner the children ate hot soup,
crusty bread and cold milk.

For dessert, they had apples
and crumbly sugar cookies.

In the evening, the sky was blue
and purple and yellow and orange and pink.

The birds were singing.
The crickets were chirping.

The children were playing.

At night, the sky was black and filled
with twinkling white stars.

The birds were dreaming.
The ants were dreaming.

The children were dreaming.

It had been just an ordinary day.
A day full of things to touch, to taste,
to see and hear and smell.
It had been just an ordinary day.
A happy just to be alive, ordinary day.